Grace-Ella

SPELLS FOR BEGINNERS

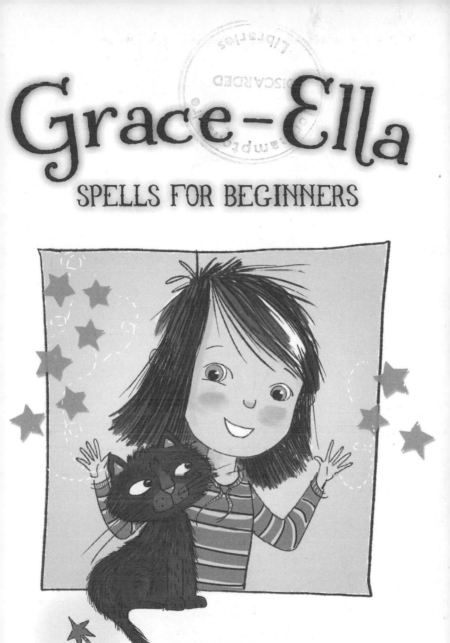

For my little boy lost

Ned x

Grace-Ella

SPELLS FOR BEGINNERS

Sharon Marie Jones

Illustrated by
Adriana J Puglisi

Firefly

First published in 2015 by Firefly Press
25 Gabalfa Road, Llandaff North, Cardiff, CF14 2JJ
www.fireflypress.co.uk

Text © Sharon Marie Jones
Illustrations © Adriana Juárez Puglisi

The author and illustrator assert their moral right to be
identified as author and illustrator in accordance with the
Copyright, Designs and Patent Act, 1988.

A CIP catalogue record of this book is available
from the British Library.

ISBN 9781910080429
ebook ISBN 9781910080436

*This book has been published with the
support of the Welsh Books Council.*

Designed by Claire Brisley

Printed and bound by Pulsio Sarl

Contents

Chapter One
The Black Cat

It all began when the black cat strolled into Number 32, Tŷ Mynydd Close. The Bevin family were eating tea when the cat ambled through the back door, past the kitchen table, and curled up on the living-room rug.

Mrs Bevin sat open-mouthed at the cheek of it. Mr Bevin wiped up the last of his gravy with some bread and butter and didn't notice. Grace-Ella felt bubbles of excitement fizzing in her tummy.

Pulling herself together, Mrs Bevin scurried after the black cat. 'Shoo! Shoo!' she shouted, flapping like a crazed chicken.

The black cat peered lazily at Mrs Bevin, yawned and snuggled back down on the rug. Following her mother into the living room, Grace-Ella began to giggle.

'This is not a laughing matter,' snapped Mrs Bevin. 'This is not a cattery. Who does he think he is waltzing in here like it's a cat hotel?'

(You see, Iona Bevin was very particular. Ever since her husband had traced her family tree and found out that she was descended from a twelfth-century prince, she thought herself rather important.)

'Now that I know I'm royalty, Bevin is a far too ordinary name, don't you think?' she'd said to her husband. Mrs Bevin had decided that she would no longer be plain old Iona Bevin, but by drawing out the last vowel, had become the rather grander-sounding Mrs Iona Bevan.)

Grace-Ella knelt to stroke the cat. He purred.

'That's not helping,' barked Mrs Bevin,

becoming increasingly hot and bothered. 'Selwyn, will you come in here and get rid of this cat!'

Mr Bevin liked a quiet life. Having decided that being a History teacher wasn't the job for him, he now owned a small bookshop in the seaside town of Aberbetws and spent his days happily reading and straightening the books on the shelves. Mr Bevin's bookshop was always bustling during the summer. Aberbetws attracted many tourists with its sandy beach and hidden coves, and visitors were always interested in old tales of local smugglers.

Despite being a bit of a historian himself, Mr Bevin didn't really like to be bothered by too many questions, and he would usually tell people to try the internet to find their answers.

He wasn't particularly bothered by a black

cat on the living-room rug either.

'Selwyn!' shrieked Mrs Bevin. 'Don't just stand there. Do something.'

'You can't throw him out,' Grace-Ella pleaded. 'He might not have a home. Or he might be lost. He won't be able to find his way in the dark. Can we let him stay, just for tonight? Please?'

Mrs Bevin looked at Mr Bevin. Mr Bevin shrugged. Mrs Bevin sighed in that way of hers.

'One night,' she said, 'then tomorrow we'll put a poster in the shop window and his rightful owner can come and get him.'

Mrs Bevin stalked back into the kitchen.

Mr Bevin smiled at his daughter, picked up his newspaper and turned on the television.

'I'm going to call you Mr Whiskins,' Grace-Ella whispered to the cat.

The following morning, Mr Bevin left for work with strict instructions to place a 'Lost Cat' poster in the bookshop window.

'Under no circumstance will that cat stay another night,' said Mrs Bevin as he climbed into his car.

Grace-Ella spent the day dreading the phone ringing or a knock at the door. She was already quite attached to Mr Whiskins. They were happily snuggled up on the sofa when there came a sudden shriek from the kitchen.

'Dead body!'

Grace-Ella raced down the hallway already suspecting that one of the neighbours would be reporting a murder. She found her mother standing on a chair pointing at a mouse – a very dead looking mouse. Oh dear, she thought. It was beginning to look like Mr Whiskins wasn't going to get on very well with her mother.

Following the immediate disposal of the dead mouse, peace was once again restored at Number 32 and the rest of the day passed uneventfully. Mr Bevin returned from work and told his wife that yes he had remembered to put the poster in the shop window.

'Well, no one has called,' she snapped. 'I shall have to phone the police.'

Mr Bevin was about to say that this wasn't really a matter for the police, but thought better of it.

Mrs Bevin picked up the phone and dialled 999.

'Police, please. I need assistance with getting rid of a cat…Yes, a cat… Bury it in the back garden? No, no, the cat's not dead. It's curled up in front of the fire… Pardon? No, this is not a hoax call and I'm certainly not wasting your time. My name is Iona Bevan and I need you to get rid… Hello? Hello?'

She stared at the phone then banged it against the table.

'Hello?' she shouted once more. 'Can you believe it? They've hung up on me. Here we are, law-abiding people who pay all our taxes, and in our hour of need they put the phone down on us. Well, I shall be writing to the Prime Minister about this.'

Mr Bevan was about to say that perhaps the police had a real emergency to sort out, but thought better of it.

'Maybe someone will call tomorrow,' Grace-Ella suggested, her fingers crossed tightly behind her back.

But much to her delight, no one called the next day, or the day after, or the day after that. A whole week passed and not one person asked about the cat. By now, Grace-Ella had fallen in love with Mr Whiskins. And it was pretty clear that Mr Whiskins was smitten with her too.

Mr Bevin had also become fond of the cat. He liked the way it sat at his feet purring quietly as he watched the television. Of course, he would never admit that to his wife.

That Saturday evening, when they were settling down to watch a DVD, bowls of popcorn on their laps, Grace-Ella felt it was the perfect time to raise the issue.

'Mam, Dad,' she began, then took a deep breath so that she could finish what she had to say before her mother interrupted her. 'I've always wanted a pet and Mr Whiskins would be perfect. He'd be no bother. I'll take care of him. And a cat's far less trouble than a dog, but far more fun than a goldfish and you'll barely notice he's here and he's been ever such a good cat since the dead mouse and as no one has come to claim him, I was wondering if I could keep him?'

Mrs Bevin looked at Mr Bevin. Mr Bevin shrugged. Mrs Bevin sighed in that way of hers.

'Well, all right … but any mess, any more dead bodies and he will be zooming off to the RSPCA shelter quicker than he can say puss puss!'

Grace-Ella leapt onto her mother, giving her a ginormous hug, sending a shower of popcorn to the floor. Mr Bevin stretched down to pat the purring cat, with a rather silly grin on his face.

Later that night, with the cat curled up at the foot of her bed, Grace-Ella couldn't stop smiling. 'Mr Whiskins, we're going to have the best fun together,' she said.

Grace-Ella had no idea just how much
fun it was going to be.

Chapter Two
At the Stroke of Midnight

If you had been on Tŷ Mynyddd Close that same night, you would have been amazed.

An ominous thundercloud hovered directly above Number 32 all evening. At the stroke of midnight, a flash of green lightning struck the house. In that second, if you'd happened to look up at Grace-Ella's bedroom window, you would have seen a black cat standing on his hind legs, his front legs swaying in the air and his green eyes ablaze.

In the blink of an eye, Number 32 returned to its sleepy state and nothing but a light breeze shuffled the leaves of the trees on Tŷ Mynydd Close.

Grace-Ella woke up the next morning feeling a little peculiar. She lay very still, then shook her head and rubbed her eyes.

'Good morning,' she said, tickling Mr Whiskins behind his ears as she climbed out of bed. 'I had a really strange dream last night. Must have been the cheese and crackers I ate for supper. Mam always says that eating cheese at bedtime gives you nightmares.'

'A good morning it is indeed,' replied an unfamiliar voice.

She spun around to see who was there. Her room was empty.

'I really shouldn't have eaten that cheese for supper,' she muttered.

'Nothing to do with the cheese,' said the voice again.

She glanced around and peered under her bed.

'It's me, Mr Whiskins. And what a splendibob name you've given me. Gives me an air of importance, don't you think?'

Grace-Ella gawped at Mr Whiskins then quickly scrunched her eyes closed and took a deep breath.

'I'm dreaming, that's all. I'm still asleep in my bed and any second now I'll wake up and everything will be just as it always is.' She slowly opened one eye and then the other.

'You're not sleeping, and nothing will ever be just as it always was, ever again,' said Mr Whiskins.

'You … but … how … cats don't talk … cats purr and miaow,' Grace-Ella stuttered.

'Ah, but I'm no ordinary cat.'

'But … I don't understand…'

'Sit down and I'll explain,' he said, patting the bed with his paw. 'You, Grace-Ella, have a gift and you are about to embark on a journey of mystery and magic.'

'This cannot be happening. I'm going completely crazy,' said Grace-Ella, 'because cats can't talk and it all sounds like riddles to me anyway.'

'Let me finish and all will come clear.'

Mr Whiskins cleared his throat and raised his head as if he was about to give a royal speech. 'You are about to discover the truth about yourself. But once the secret is revealed, there will be no turning back...'

He paused. Grace-Ella nervously nodded for him to continue.

'Very well. You, Grace-Ella, are … a witch.'

'A witch?' she spluttered. 'Don't be silly. Where's my pointy hat and broomstick? Where's my black … oh.'

She was about to add 'cat', but realised that she did indeed have a black cat, sitting right in front of her.

'A witch! Really!'

'Yes, Grace-Ella, you are a witch. Witchcraft has been in your family for generations. Your Great-Grandmother, Olwen, was a witch. Your mother's cousin, Nesta, is also a witch. And you were born during the year of the black cat and as today is the ninth day of the ninth month of the ninth year of your life, you have been bestowed with the powers of witchcraft.'

Grace-Ella's urge to laugh turned into a prickly feeling at the back of her neck.

'Are you saying there are lots of witches around?' she asked.

'Witches are everywhere. They pass you on the street. They sit next to you on the bus.'

'But witches are dressed in black and wear hats and fly around on broomsticks. I would have noticed them.'

'Those are the witches in stories and at Halloween parties, they're not real witches,' explained Mr Whiskins.

'So how can you tell if someone's a real witch?'

'It's not too difficult, once you know what to look for. For a start, a witch has that something a little bit different about her. Something that you can't quite put your finger on. A niggling that makes you want to stop and stare.'

Grace-Ella thought about this. Since she was born, people had commented on her bright, green eyes and her shock of black hair, especially as both Mr and Mrs Bevin had fair hair and blue eyes. She supposed that this could be seen as a little odd, and it certainly did made people look twice.

'Take a peek at a witch's feet and you will see that they are outward pointing,' continued Mr Whiskins.

Grace-Ella peered at her feet and noticed that they were slightly outward pointing. Maybe this explained why she was not very good at sports and why her PE teacher, Miss Fitz, always wrote in her school report that she seemed to have two left feet.

'A witch's hands move quickly, as on the palm of their left hand hides a green five-pointed star.'

Grace-Ella breathed a sigh of relief. She turned her left palm upwards to prove to Mr Whiskins that he had made a terrible mistake … then screamed.

There, as bold as your nose, was a small, yet perfectly formed glimmering green five-pointed star.

'And of course,' Mr Whiskins ended, 'every witch has a black cat. You have a magnifulous gift. Magic in the tips of your fingers…'

'A witch,' Grace-Ella whispered, staring at the star on her hand. 'I suppose I've always known I was a bit different.'

Grace-Ella had never really felt like a traditional little girl. She would kick and scream when her mother tried to dress her in anything pink and frilly and insisted on wearing dark purple or black.

She'd been expelled from her first ballet

lesson for biting Madame Monique when she tried to pull on her tutu.

She wasn't scared of the dark or creepy-crawlies and would set spiders out gently in the back garden when she found one in the house.

She sometimes found a frog in the garden pond and would put it in the bathtub to

keep as a pet. Only the other week, Mrs Bevin had found one just as she was about to have a relaxing, bubbly soak before bed. Horrified, she had phoned Environmental Health, demanding that they come at once to get rid of the slithery thing.

Grace-Ella was happiest out in the back garden, playing with Bedwyr from next door. They collected bugs to keep in Bedwyr's shed for his scientific experiments. He dissected the bugs then looked up their anatomy on his computer, hence his nickname, Bedwyr Bug-Buster. It had caused Mrs Bevin great distress to see her daughter come into the house, hands caked in mud and clothes smeared with dirt.

'Grace-Ella,' she would say despairingly, 'little girls don't roll around in mud. Little girls are nice and sweet and pretty. It's that ghastly boy's influence, that's what it is.'

Mrs Bevin was utterly baffled and couldn't understand what on earth she had done wrong. She took Grace-Ella to the doctor and after having every test imaginable done, a disgruntled Mrs Bevin was told that her daughter was a perfectly normal, healthy little girl.

On Grace-Ella's fifth birthday, a beaming Mrs Bevin enrolled her daughter at St Winifred's Private Girls' School, determined that she would become a perfect young lady (as was fitting for a royal descendant).

Mr Bevin couldn't understand why his wife insisted on paying for their daughter to attend a school ten miles away. He had wanted to say that she would do just fine at the local school, but he thought better of it.

So Grace-Ella being a witch did actually

explain a lot of things.

'What should I do now?' she asked Mr Whiskins.

'You'll have to tell your parents. But I have a wiggling in my whiskers that your mother isn't going to take the news too well.'

Mr and Mrs Bevin were sitting at the kitchen table. Mr Bevin was about to say good morning, but Mrs Bevin began to speak before he'd had the chance.

'What were you screaming about up there? Don't tell me, that cat left you a nice present on your bed. I knew it wouldn't take him long to start showing his true colours. Well, you know what I said, any mess…'

'Mam, Dad,' Grace-Ella began, interrupting her mother's outburst. 'There's something important we need to tell you.'

Chapter Three
The Secret Revealed

'A witch!' shrieked Mrs Bevin. 'A witch! That is the most ridiculous thing I've ever heard. It's all this commercial Halloween nonsense, that's what it is. Don't tell me, you're going to insist on going to school tomorrow in a witch's costume and you won't be needing a lift, as you'll be flying there on your broomstick.'

Mrs Bevin looked at Mr Bevin. Mr Bevin shrugged. Mrs Bevin sighed in that way of hers. 'Say something, Selwyn,' she hissed.

'Perhaps we should listen to what they have to say?' he suggested.

'They? They? That is a cat sitting on your daughter's lap. Unless you've turned into Dr Dolittle overnight, you can't talk to a cat.'

'Ah, but you are mistaken,' said Mr

Whiskins.

Mrs Bevin leapt out of her chair with a window-shattering scream.

Mr Bevin leaned forward, more animated than he'd ever been in his entire life.

'Let me explain,' said Mr Whiskins.

Neither Mrs Bevin nor Mr Bevin blinked as Mr Whiskins told them about the generations of witches in the family.

'So you see,' he ended, 'if you look again at your family tree, you'll find not only royalty in your blood, but also witchcraft. And as Grace-Ella was born in the year of the black cat, she is now a witch.'

Mrs Bevin turned incredibly pale. She tried to speak but no sound came out.

Mr Bevin was completely flummoxed – how on earth had he missed this vital information when researching their family tree?

'I suppose,' Mrs Bevin finally spoke in a quavery voice, 'this does explain why Granny Olwen was such a wicked old hag.'

'My Great Grandfather was Granny Olwen's black cat,' said Mr Whiskins, 'and he didn't have a bad word to say against her.'

Mrs Bevin narrowed her eyes. 'Bottletops. I remember the horrible thing. He was always hissing and baring his teeth at me.'

'It doesn't matter what Granny Olwen

was like,' interrupted Grace-Ella. 'What's important is that I'm a witch. And it does explain a lot, doesn't it?'

Iona Bevin was dumbfounded. She had always felt that there was something terribly wrong with her daughter, but this was too much.

'This is awful,' she snivelled. 'What am I going to do? I'll be an outcast. I'll have to become a recluse. We'll have to move away … somewhere remote … a shack on top of the highest mountain…'

'Perhaps it's not as bad as you think,' said Mr Bevin.

Grace-Ella turned eagerly to her father.

'Now you won't need to worry about why Grace-Ella sometimes struggles to fit in. We know now that she's not different, she's gifted. I think we're very lucky to have such a special daughter,' he said smiling.

Mrs Bevin dabbed delicately at her eyes with her scarf. 'Will she have to attend a special witch school?' she asked.

'No, Grace-Ella will learn witchcraft herself,' said Mr Whiskins. 'We don't want witches to close themselves away from everyone else. Her first package should arrive today. She can go to Witch Camp and there are the annual WCAs, the Witch Council Awards, which you can attend as a family.'

As she listened to Mr Whiskins talking, Grace-Ella began to have a heavy sinking feeling in the pit of her stomach.

'What if I'm no good at being a witch?' she asked quietly. 'Mam often says I'm not the brightest grape in the bunch and I never have glowing school reports.'

'That's because you've never had the chance to shine. You wait and see. I bet you become a magnifulous-splendifulous witch,' said Mr Whiskins.

Grace-Ella smiled.

'And what kind of future will my daughter have as a … a witch?' asked Mrs Bevin.

'Well, think of Harmony Enchanta, the world-famous perfumer. I think you wear her perfume, '*Enchanted*'? She is a witch, of course.'

Mrs Bevin perked up. 'Harmony Enchanta?'

'And the fashion designer, Serena Starling,' continued Mr Whiskins. '*Serena's designs, sprinkled with magic.*'

'Blimey,' said Mrs Bevin. 'I had no idea. So Grace-Ella could be world-famous one day? Imagine what Anne will say to that. She's forever going on about how her Amelia is more than ready for university, as she's been reading fluently since the

age of two. Worldwide fame, now that is something worth boasting about.'

'Perhaps we shouldn't tell anyone,' said Grace-Ella. 'I don't want everyone pointing at me in school and whispering behind my back. They think I'm odd enough as it is.'

'Grace-Ella's right,' said Mr Whiskins. 'This must be kept a family secret.'

He pounced suddenly to the floor and slowly circled the room. The Bevins edged forwards in their chairs, watching his every move.

'Remember that there could be eyes and ears lurking anywhere,' he whispered.

'I can put you straight right now,' snapped Mrs Bevin, shattering the air of mystery. 'There's nothing lurking in my house. Not a cobweb in sight. But I suppose you're right. It'll be best to keep it a secret. People can be very ignorant about this sort of thing, very narrow-minded. And I doubt very much that a witch would be accepted at St Winifred's. Yes, my lips shall remain sealed.'

Mr Bevin nearly said that they'd be more likely to see a pig fly, but thought better of it.

The doorbell rang, stopping them all.

'I sense your first package,' said Mr Whiskins. 'I have a tingling in my tail.'

Bursting with excitement, Grace-Ella ran to the front door.

'Parcels for Miss Grace-Ella Bevin,' announced the postman. 'Sign here, please.'

Grace-Ella carefully signed and balanced the brown paper parcels precariously in her arms. Wanting to give her parents space to digest her news, knowing that her mother was still in shock and needed a strong coffee, she tottered up to her bedroom to open them.

Chapter Four
The Book of Rules

Grace-Ella opened the first parcel and found a small touch-screen tablet inside. She turned it on and after a few seconds of whirring, the blank screen lit up. 'Welcome to The Witch Academy' flashed across, before it turned black again. She tapped the screen a few times, but nothing happened. She was beginning to think that it must be broken when an image started to appear. A tall woman dressed in a long, black cloak, with snow-white hair cut sharply at her chin and small half-moon glasses balancing at the end of her nose, stepped out of the screen and stood in the middle of the bedroom like a hologram.

'Good morning,' she said crisply, peering over her glasses. 'My name is Penelope

Pendle and I am the head of the Witch Council. As you are aware, you are now officially a witch and it's of paramount importance that you strictly follow the Council's rules. Failure to do this could have dire consequences for yourself and your future as a witch. You must read and learn *The Book of Rules* before you begin your training. Now, unless you have any urgent questions I shall leave you and, all being well, won't see you again until you're ready for Witch Camp.'

Grace-Ella sat on her bed in stunned silence, her mouth gaping open.

'Excellent,' announced Penelope Pendle, before vanishing in a puff of purple smoke.

'She was in a hurry,' said Mr Whiskins. 'Lots of witchy work to do, I suppose. Come on, let's open the other packages.'

In the second parcel was a wooden box.

Grace-Ella carefully lifted the lid and inside was a wooden wand. Circling the widest end was a ring of black and emerald gem stones, which twisted halfway up the wand like a creeping vine. At its tip was a five-pointed star.

Lying on top of the wand was a small rectangular card with strange black

symbols written on it.

'I wonder what they mean,' puzzled Grace-Ella.

She turned the card over and on the other side in bold black letters was the word 'BESTOW'.

'It must be the name of my wand,' she whispered. 'The symbols must be the magical way of writing it.'

Grace-Ella's heart beat quicker as she held the wand in her hands. Had she really been bestowed with magical powers? Would she be able to cast real spells?

Placing the wand back in its box, she unwrapped the next parcel: a book. Its cover was dark purple velvet with the words '*The Book of Rules* by Aldyth Bedortha' written in shimmering gold.

The last and heaviest of the packages was a small black cauldron.

'Wow,' said Grace-Ella gazing at her new gifts. 'I really am a witch.'

Settling back against her pillows, she picked up *The Book of Rules*. She turned to the first page, which was written in an old-fashioned black twirling font. She was about to start reading, but the book started to read itself in a shrill high-pitched voice. Resting it on her lap, Grace-Ella listened.

"Greetings, fellow witch. My name is Aldyth Bedortha and I am the founder of the Witch Academy. You are now a member and you must abide by 'The Nine Golden Rules'. Failure to keep to these rules will result in punishment or even banishment from the witch community. Read on for case studies of witches who broke the rules and follow their example at your peril. You have been warned."

The Nine Golden Rules

Rule 1: Always cast your magic in private.
Only in the company of other witches
can spells be cast openly.

Rule 2: Never use your magic as a means of reveng
on a foe. Your magic is to be used for good only.

Rule 3: Never allow personal greed to affect your
magic. Your magic cannot be used as a means of
making you rich.

Rule 4: Never use your magic to cheat.
You must not cast spells to help you to cheat in any
circumstance, as you must continue to learn life's skill
and lessons in the same manner as ordinary folk.

Rule 5: Never use your magic on unsuspecting
victims. A person should always be aware that magic
being cast on them.

Rule 6: Do not exceed nine spells on one person. A non-witch has a spell limit of nine. Exceeding nine spells will result in permanent changes to that person.

Rule 7: Never cast a spell on another witch. Casting a spell on another witch tampers greatly with her powers and can be extremely dangerous.

Rule 8: Always follow spells and potions carefully. Do not attempt to alter an established spell or potion – the results could be disastrous.

Rule 9: Report mistakes immediately. If you cast a wrong spell, or a spell doesn't work as it should, you must report the incident to the Witch Council, who will then manage the situation.

Abide by 'The Nine Golden Rules' and you shall become a successful witch.

Good luck.

The book banged itself shut, startling Grace-Ella. She really was going to have to get used to all these strange happenings if she was to become a successful witch.

That night Grace-Ella lay awake long after she heard her parents go to bed. She was far too excited to sleep. Tomorrow she would have to suffer a whole day in school, now that the summer holidays were over, before she could return home and start casting her first spells.

Grace-Ella had never really liked school. She envied the way Bedwyr talked about his school – smiley teachers and fun lessons. He once asked her what they did during 'Friday's Golden Hour' at St Winifred's. Once he had explained what he meant, Grace-Ella had answered, 'Oh, if we've worked hard all week we're allowed half an hour free time to practise the harp or traditional dancing.'

'You're hilarious,' he'd said, clearly thinking that she was joking.

Tucking her wand under her pillow, Grace-Ella finally drifted off to sleep. That night, her dreams were filled with tall witches with shrill voices and puffs of purple smoke.

Chapter Five
Spells for Beginners

At breakfast the following morning, Mrs Bevin worried about what she was supposed to do with the cat all day.

'I'll be out all morning. I've got yoga and then a skinny-latte and catch-up with the girls. I hope you can keep yourself out of mischief,' she said, glaring at Mr Whiskins.

'You know what we cats say – while the boss is away, bring the mice out to play,' he teased.

Mrs Bevin inhaled sharply, her cheeks flushed and her nostrils flared. She opened her mouth to say something, but couldn't think of a reply.

Mr Bevin smiled. He'd tried to have the last word in conversations with his wife for years. He looked at the cat in awe.

Mr Bevin dropped Grace-Ella off at the school gates then drove the ten miles back along the narrow country road to Aberbetws.

St Winifred's was an imposing, grey stone building, built on a hillside. It had two large archways at the front. Between the arches was a large plaque with the name of the school and the date it opened, 1847, inscribed on it.

Under one archway, the younger girls lined up, with the older girls queuing at the other. Grace-Ella always thought that they looked like long slithery snakes dressed in their hideous bottle-green pinafores.

She pushed open the heavy iron gates and walked up the winding driveway edged with trees. She headed straight towards her friend, Fflur Penri. Fflur was also a bit of a loner and they had quickly become best friends.

Fflur was constantly being teased at school by Amelia and her friends. They had given her the nickname 'Fatty Fflur'. She was a little bit big, which seemed to be a Penri family trait. Mrs Penri prepared big, hearty meals and puddings for her husband and didn't think twice about piling up her daughter's plate as well. Fflur often returned home from school upset about Amelia's spiteful words, but Mrs Penri would simply say, 'Ffluri-fach, it's only a little puppy fat. Don't listen to those horrid girls. You're lovely just as you are. Come on, let's make some buttery pancakes for tea.'

At lunchtime, Fflur and Grace-Ella were sitting on one of the benches under the trees.

'Oh no,' groaned Grace-Ella. 'What does she want now?'

Tip-tapping towards them with her long

hair swishing around her shoulders was Amelia. With her head held high and her nose pointed in the air, she looked like a wily fox sniffing out its prey.

'Miss Fitz has asked me to tell everyone to bring their PE kits every day next week, as there'll be hockey practice every lunchtime. There's a friendly match next Saturday

against St Clare's and she wants to choose a team. Not that you have any chance of being picked. Oh, and by the way, Grace-Ella, Mami says she hopes that new flea-ball cat of yours is kept locked indoors at night because she doesn't want to find any poopies on our front lawn.'

Smiling tightly and rolling her eyes in disgust at Fflur, she turned on her heels and marched off.

'Ugh, she's such a horror. And that whiny voice of hers gives me the googies. Perhaps I'll tell Mr Whiskins to leave a little present on number fifteen's doorstep,' giggled Grace-Ella.

'What was that?' asked Fflur, wiping the crumbs of her smuggled pastry from her mouth.

'Nothing,' Grace-Ella replied as the bell rang.

*

'I know who I'll be casting my first spell on,' Grace-Ella told Mr Whiskins that evening. 'I'm going to turn Miss Snooty-nosed Amelia into a bug and squish her under my shoe.'

'Be careful,' warned Mr Whiskins. 'Remember the second rule.'

Sighing, Grace-Ella sat at her desk and started up the tablet. She opened the file 'Spells for Beginners' and read 'Spell Number 1'.

A simple spell to get you on your way,
Let's turn your room from night to day.
Turn off the lights and close your eyes,
Then say the words for a bright surprise.

Grace-Ella re-read the spell until she was certain that she could remember it then turned off her bedroom light, closed her eyes and waved her magic wand.

'Flick, click, turn on the light. Change this room from dark to bright.'

She opened her eyes and squealed: the light in her room was switched on again. 'I did it! I cast my first spell and it worked.'

She eagerly turned to 'Spell Number 2'.

A useful spell for clearing a mess,
As tidying up we will address.
On the floor place a cup,
Then say the words for it to rise up.

Placing an empty cup on the floor she waved her wand once more.

'This way, that way, twirl with grace. Return the cup to its rightful place.'

A flash of light sparked at the end of her wand and she watched in amazement as the cup slowly lifted from the floor. It hovered in front of her face, before gliding gently to the bedside table.

'What did I tell you?' said Mr Whiskins. 'You're going to be a magnifulous-splendifulous witch.'

Grace-Ella felt like there were hundreds of fluttery butterflies in her stomach. She never got her schoolwork right on the first go. She always had to rewrite her stories while Mrs Nag loudly chanted, 'Capital letters and full stops, capital letters and full stops.' And when she got her Maths work back, she could always expect a bright array of red crosses scattered across her page.

By the time Grace-Ella went to bed that night, she had watched her books bounce back onto the shelf, her pens and pencils pop back into their pots and her dirty clothes dance delightfully into the wash basket.

At eight o'clock Mrs Bevin came upstairs, as she did every night, to say goodnight and to sigh in that way of hers at the mess in her daughter's room.

'Grace-Ella, a young lady's bedroom should be neat and tidy, not a grotty hovel like this…'

'A very nice grotty hovel, don't you think?' said Mr Whiskins.

Mrs Bevin stared at her daughter's perfectly neat bedroom, her mouth opening and closing silently like a goldfish. Shaking her head, she muttered, 'Goodnight,' and left the room, banging the door behind her.

'That was a real magical moment,' said

Grace-Ella, laughing. 'I'm going to have so much fun being a witch. I can't wait to have a go at casting more spells.'

Chapter Six
Slugs, Mice and All Things Nice

It was a damp and drizzly Saturday morning. Grace-Ella was looking forward to two days of magic and had decided to try mixing her first potion.

Mrs Bevin had booked herself into the newly opened spa in Aberbetws. Mr Bevin had decided not to open the shop and was going to spend the morning burrowing like a beaver through the weekend's newspapers.

'I'm a bit nervous about mixing my first potion,' Grace-Ella said, peering into the gleaming black cauldron.

'There's no need to be,' Mr Whiskins replied. 'Every spell that you've tried so far has been perfect.'

Grace-Ella beamed. She couldn't believe

that she had managed to cast several of the 'Spells for Beginners' without making any mistakes.

She opened the file 'Potions: Part One' and skimmed quickly down the contents list – Bursting Boils and Bunions, Farewell Facial Fur, Give the Giggles, Got the Giggles, Halting Hiccups and Worrying Warts were a few that caught her eye.

'Some of these sound pretty gross.'

She finally decided to have a go at the Halting Hiccups potion.

'It'll be useful, if I get it right. I had a really bad bout of hiccups last week, right in the middle of Mrs Nag's Welsh lesson. She made me stand outside until they'd stopped and then I had to have the lesson by myself during break. But I suppose I'll have to magic up a potion to give me the hiccups first.'

'Firstly, I need some sticky slug slime and three hairs from a mouse,' she said.

Mr Whiskins scampered off then returned with the ingredients and in they were plopped.

'A teaspoon of cuckoo spit, five rotting sprouts and a bath bomb to add some fizz,' she added.

She stirred the potion with a large

wooden spoon and watched delighted as it brewed and bubbled from yellow to brown to green.

'Look, it's bubbling up all by itself,' she said in wonderment.

'That's the power of magic,' said Mr Whiskins. 'Now say the magic words.'

'Bubble and boil and stir it all up. Brew me a magical hiccupy hiccup.'

As she poured some of the liquid into a glass, bubbles darted from the bottom and foam fizzed over the brim.

'If this doesn't give me the hiccups, I don't know what will. Now I'll leave it to cool in the fridge and get on with the Halting Hiccups potion.'

'Grace-Ella, lunch is ready,' Mrs Bevin called from the bottom of the stairs a little later. Grace-Ella walked into the kitchen and froze. The glass of hiccupy potion was in her mother's hand.

'Very kind of Dad to make me one of these health shakes,' she said, sniffing at the potion. 'It's got a rather nasty smell to it.'

'Mam…'

Grace-Ella's eyes widened in horror as her mother held onto her nose and gulped down the whole glass.

'Ghastly! Now where is that father of yours? And do sit down, Grace-Ella. You're standing there like a gawping gibbon.'

Mrs Bevin scooted out of the kitchen calling for her husband.

'What am I going to do?' Grace-Ella said.

'We'll just have to wait and see what happens,' Mr Whiskins replied.

Mr Whiskins was right. She'd just have to see what effect the potion would have on her mother. It was her first attempt so it probably wouldn't even work, she thought.

The Bevins sat at the kitchen table eating their lunch of tuna salad sandwiches. Every so often Grace-Ella glanced at her mother to see if anything unusual was happening.

'I had the seaweed wrap at the spa. It's meant to be very good for the skin … hic…'

Grace-Ella paused, her sandwich hovering mid-way to her mouth.

'That health … hic … shake … hic … seems to be having a rather … hic … gassy effect on … hic … me. What did you … hic … put in it … hic?'

'Health shake?' asked Mr Bevin frowning.

'Yes, the one you … hic … left in the fridge … hic?'

'I don't know what you're talking about,' said Mr Bevin, clearly confused.

Grace-Ella squirmed in her seat as her mother's hiccups grew louder.

'The … HIC … health … HIC … shake … HIC!'

With that final hiccup, Mrs Bevin rose from her chair.

'What … HIC … on earth … HIC … is going on … HIC?' she shouted as with each hiccup she rose higher into the air.

Mr Bevin stared at his wife. He had no idea what was happening.

Her hiccupping grew louder and louder and she rose higher and higher until she bumped her head on the ceiling.

'Um … I think I should explain,' began Grace-Ella. 'I was trying out some potions and I thought I'd have a go at Halting Hiccups. I made up a potion that would give me the hiccups so that I could see if it worked. It wasn't a health shake that you drank, it was my hiccuppy potion. And I was only going to take a sip, not drink the whole glass.'

'Sel … HIC … wyn!' Mrs Bevin shrieked. 'Do … HIC … something … HIC!'

'I'm sure Grace-Ella has everything under control,' Mr Bevin said, looking anxiously at his daughter.

'Under … HIC … control … HIC! Can't you … HIC … see … HIC … that I'm … HIC … stuck to the … HIC … ceiling!'

'Don't worry,' said Grace-Ella, leaping from her chair. 'The Halting Hiccups potion is ready. Just hang on for a minute, I'll be right back.'

Mrs Bevin didn't have much choice.

Grace-Ella raced back down the stairs with a glass of bright red liquid in her hand.

'Here it is. Drink this.'

'How … HIC … may I ask … HIC … are you going to get the blinkin' thing … HIC

'… up to me … HIC?'

'Um … well … maybe if I stand on the chair and Mr Whiskins stands on my shoulders, he could stretch up and you could grab the drink?'

'Always ready to help a damsel in distress,' said Mr Whiskins, bowing his head gallantly.

Mrs Bevin looked at Mr Bevin. Mr Bevin shrugged. Mrs Bevin sighed in that way of hers.

'Get a … HIC … move on then … HIC … this is … HIC … all very … HIC … undignified … HIC.'

Grace-Ella clambered onto her chair. Mr Whiskins leapt onto her shoulders and she carefully placed the glass between his front paws. They wobbled a little as Mr Whiskins stretched up as far as he could. Mrs Bevin rocked herself into a sitting position and stretched down as far as she could until she grabbed onto the glass. In one swift movement, she poured the whole glass of red liquid into her mouth.

Grace-Ella, Mr Whiskins and Mr Bevin sat at the table and waited. Mrs Bevin, lying horizontally with her back against the ceiling, closed her eyes and became very still.

After a few minutes, Mrs Bevin's face turned a sickly shade of green. Her eyes shot open and the three at the table gasped. Just as they thought she was looking normal again, she began to redden. Her face became redder and redder and redder. When they thought that she would surely explode, a hissing puff of smoke escaped from her nostrils.

'What a magnifibob sight,' said Mr Whiskins. 'She looks like a fierce dragon.'

They watched in awe as with each hissing puff, Mrs Bevin slowly descended. Down and down she came, until she was perched once more on her chair. Her face was all sooty, as if she'd just worked a shift down a coal mine. She smoothed down her hair, which had become a little frizzy from the heat.

'I'm going for a lie down,' she said quietly. 'This … this … incident has been very traumatic. I never want it mentioned again.'

Holding onto the table, she sighed in that way of hers before walking unsteadily out of the room.

The kitchen's three occupants sat in stunned silence, pondering what they'd just witnessed. Eventually, Mr Whiskins spoke.

'Another success, Grace-Ella. You truly are a magnifulous-splendifulous witch.'

'Remarkable,' added Mr Bevin.

Chapter Seven
Hockey Horrors

Mrs Bevin wasn't seen for the remainder of the weekend. She lay on her bed with an eye-mask on and the sound of the sea playing softly into her headphones.

'I'm dreading school next week,' Grace-Ella said to Mr Whiskins as she packed her books into her bag on Sunday evening. 'We have to practise hockey every day and Amelia's going to be her usual nasty self and make fun of me and Fflur.'

'You have to learn to ignore her,' said Mr Whiskins.

'It'd be far easier if I could just cast a spell and turn her into a big fat frog so that she would just ribbit off.'

She settled into bed, feeling utterly miserable at the thought of the week ahead.

Monday began with the weekly debate. Mrs Nag insisted that being able to voice their opinions clearly and confidently was very important. St Winifred's always entered the annual 'School Debating Championships' and were currently the reigning champions.

Grace-Ella had never quite got over her first experience at debating, during her first term at St Winifred's. Mrs Nag had written up that morning's question on the board. Grace-Ella, who was struggling to learn to read well, squinted at the words, trying her very best to decipher them.

'Grace-Ella, you can start us off today,' Mrs Nag had said.

Grace-Ella walked nervously to the front of the class.

'Um … I don't think that it's important to have gross beef dinner because most vegetables are yucky and we should be allowed to eat delicious food like pizza every day.'

A classroom of confused faces stared back at Grace-Ella. She felt heat slowly rising from her neck to her face.

Frowning, Mrs Nag said, 'What are you talking about?'

'Um … the debate question. Is it important to have gross beef dinner?'

An explosion of laughter erupted in the class like a volcano. Mrs Nag closed her eyes and shook her head.

'That's enough class. Enough!' she shouted, trying to regain control over the giggling girls. 'Grace-Ella, what are we going to do with you? The question asks: Is it important to have grace before dinner?'

Grace-Ella walked slowly back to her table, her head bent and tears pricking her eyes. She didn't see Amelia stick her foot out as she passed. Grace-Ella fell sprawling across the floor. Quick to help her up, so that Mrs Nag could see what a kind pupil she was, Amelia smirked, 'You're such a dumb-brain, Gross-Ella!'

Ever since, Amelia did her best to confuse and embarrass Grace-Ella during the debating lessons, firing questions at her and using long obscure words that left her completely bewildered and befuddled. That morning was no different. Grace-Ella was relieved when the bell finally rang.

After lunch, the girls gathered in the changing room for hockey practice. Amelia, as usual, was busily barking her instructions at the others.

'Obviously I'm the one who'll win the game for us, so you have to make sure that you all pass the ball to me. St Clare's defence will be no match for me and I'll easily get the goals in. Ceinwen and Megan, you'll definitely get picked for defence, so you have to make sure that you don't give them a chance to score. It might just be a friendly game, but we're there to win, not to be the losers.'

Amelia turned to Grace-Ella and Fflur, who were quietly getting changed.

'There's no way that Miss Fitz is going to pick you two. Grace-Ella, you always spend more time face down in the mud than on your feet. And as for you, Fatty Fflur, you'll be out of cream puff before you even get onto the field. You should stick to a sport you'd be good at … like a custard pie eating contest.'

Amelia and her friends snorted with laughter.

'Ignore them,' whispered Grace-Ella to

Fflur, who was blushing crimson.

Just then, Amelia lunged at the bench like a swooping sparrow and snatched up Fflur's shorts.

'Give them back,' snapped Fflur.

'Come and get them, Fatty,' laughed Amelia, throwing the shorts to Ceinwen. Fflur turned and made a grab for them, just as they flew to Megan.

'You're a rotten crab apple, Amelia,' said Grace-Ella. 'Your mum should scrub your horrid nasty tongue with soap and a wire brush.'

Both Grace-Ella and Fflur swiped unsuccessfully at the shorts as they flew from one side of the room to the other. The shorts-throwing came to an abrupt halt as they heard Miss Fitz enter the changing room.

'Ready, girls?' she hollered.

Amelia quickly dropped the shorts back into Fflur's bag.

'Fflur Penri, what are you doing prancing around in your underwear?' Miss Fitz asked. 'Amelia, will you go and start the warm-ups while I wait for this pair please?'

Glancing back triumphantly, Amelia led the others onto the field.

With the warm-ups done, Miss Fitz set the girls into two teams for a practice game. Fflur ended up on Amelia's team, much to Amelia's horror. She ordered Fflur to play in goal.

'Just stand still,' she hissed. 'Your lardy jelly bottom fills the goal so you don't need to move.'

Grace-Ella actually found herself striking the ball a few times and sending it in the correct direction.

'A marked improvement, Grace-Ella,'
Miss Fitz commented at the end of
Wednesday's session. 'Keep up the good
work.'

Grace-Ella smiled proudly whilst Amelia
glowered at her.

On Friday, Miss Fitz announced the team
before the final practice.

'Amelia, you'll be captain and will play
Centre Forward. Rhiannon, Martha,
Sophie and Jessica, you'll be on the wings.

Zoe, Lucy and Catrin will play Half Backs whilst Ceinwen and Grace-Ella will play in defence. And Fflur, you'll be in goal. The rest of you will get a chance next time. And remember girls, this is a nice friendly pre-season match. We're there to have fun and enjoy the game.'

'I can't believe I didn't get picked,' whined Megan.

'Don't worry, Megan. I'll make sure that you're on the team,' said Amelia, pushing her way past Grace-Ella and Fflur.

'What did she mean by that?' wondered Fflur.

'Who knows?' answered Grace-Ella, shrugging.

For the following twenty minutes, the girls played a half-pitch game, attack against defence.

Amelia grew increasingly frustrated as Ceinwen often managed to get the ball from her before she'd had a shot at goal.

'Stop tackling me,' she snarled at her friend. 'I'm not exactly able to show myself at my best with you pouncing on me all the time.'

'But that's what I'm supposed to do,' replied Ceinwen.

'Just do what I say and let me score,' ordered Amelia.

With only a few minutes left, Grace-Ella watched as Amelia charged up the field towards them, the ball dancing beside her swiftly moving feet. Grace-Ella looked across at Ceinwen, who was pretending to tie her laces and was not going to try to tackle her friend. It was going to be down to her.

She grasped her stick tightly. Just a few

more metres and she'd lunge at the ball and swipe it away from Amelia, hopefully swiping the smile off her face in the process.

Three metres to go … two…

Closing her eyes tightly, Grace-Ella lifted her stick, swung back her arm and … thwack!

She opened her eyes to find herself face down on the ground, a searing pain in her left ankle.

'Grace-Ella, are you OK?' she heard Miss Fitz ask as she rushed over to her.

'Sorry, Miss. I thought she was going to move or block me with her stick, not swing it back like a golf club. I never would have struck so hard if I'd known,' protested Amelia innocently.

'Accidents happen, Amelia. It was nobody's fault. Let's get you into the changing room to check that ankle, Grace-Ella.'

'No serious damage, nothing broken but you'll have a nice purple bruise by tomorrow. I think it'll be best if you don't play this time,' said Miss Fitz. 'Megan, you'll have to take Grace-Ella's position on defence. Now back to class, girls, excitement over. I'll see you tomorrow at one o'clock.'

'Never mind, Grace-Ella,' Amelia sniggered. 'The best position for you was always going to be sitting on the bench.'

And with yet another triumphant smile, she strutted out of the changing room like a proud peacock.

'She did it on purpose,' said Fflur angrily, as she helped Grace-Ella to pack everything back into her bag. 'She's such a horrid old moo. I wish we could get our own back on her. She deserves a dose of her own medicine.'

'Hmm,' agreed Grace-Ella, as she hobbled back to class.

Chapter Eight
Magical Mayhem

The hockey incident was soon forgotten. Grace-Ella had secretly been pleased when St Clare's won the match, by eight goals to six. But she had felt bad for Fflur, who had to suffer a venomous attack from Amelia following the game.

As she practised her spells and potions, Grace-Ella couldn't help but wish there was some way of using her magic to teach Amelia a lesson.

Within just a few weeks, she had mastered the majority of 'Spells for Beginners' and had an impressive collection of bottled potions lined up alphabetically on the shelves in the summer house.

Mrs Bevin had been very impressed with

Tickly Tonsils and Stop Sneezing when
Mr Bevin came home one evening feeling
rotten, coughing and sneezing non-stop.
Mrs Bevin had shooed him straight to
the spare bedroom to contain the germs,
wrapping a scarf around her face whenever
she took him any food and drink.

Mr Bevin wanted to say that he only had a cold, not some dreadful tropical disease, but thought better of it.

When the potions were ready, Mr Bevin gulped them down willingly and within a few minutes, was fit and healthy, not a cough or a sneeze in sight.

'Incredible, Grace-Ella,' Mrs Bevin beamed. 'You really are good at all this witchy-witchiness. How very clever you are.'

Grace-Ella couldn't quite believe that her mother had used her name and the word 'clever' in the same sentence. Now that really was incredible.

She was having such a good time being a witch that she desperately wanted to share her secret with her best friends. She hated keeping the truth from them and she really wanted them to be a part of the fun. But she worried that they wouldn't believe her and would think that she'd completely lost the plot. And even if they did believe her, what if they didn't want a witch as a friend? What if they thought that she was too weird and stayed away from her? She was in a peppered pickle over the whole thing.

'Fflur's coming to play tomorrow,' Grace-Ella told her parents one Friday evening.

'You could have given me more warning,' sighed Mrs Bevin. 'I haven't done the food shop yet and she's always so hungry. Well, it won't do her any harm to cut down for the day. She's a lovely girl, just so over … over-fed.'

Fflur was dropped off at Number 32, at ten o'clock the following morning.

'She's got some homemade Welsh cakes in her bag, just in case the girls get hungry,'

Mrs Penri told Mrs Bevin. 'Shall I pick her up, say, five?'

'What do you want to do?' asked Fflur as she and Grace-Ella sat in the back garden.

Before Grace-Ella had a chance to reply, they heard a shuffling and scraping from the other side of the fence. Up popped Bedwyr, fully dressed in his bug-busting gear – a green jumper with brown leather

patches on the elbows, camouflage trousers, a black, fur-rim deerstalker hat and swimming goggles (which he insisted gave him X-ray vision).

'Is the coast clear? No dangerous Snootyius Ladyiums lurking in the area?' he asked.

'All clear,' Grace-Ella giggled. 'Jump over.'

'Snootyius Ladyiums?' asked a puzzled Fflur.

'That's his scientific name for Mam,' explained Grace-Ella.

Bedwyr landed in the garden, glanced at the back door then dashed across to the girls.

'Ok, here's the plan,' he said. 'I need to find a *Hypothenemus Obscurus*.'

'A Hypotty-what?' asked Grace-Ella.

'It's a beetle to you. An "Apple Twig Beetle" to be exact.'

Grace-Ella was always amazed at how Bedwyr knew the name of every bug that lived on the planet. His ambition in life was to find an undiscovered bug and name it himself.

'So where will we find these hypotty-beetles?' asked Fflur.

'Mainly in the US,' answered Bedwyr, grinning. 'But you never know. We might just strike lucky. We could become famous for being the first to find one out of its native land.'

'You're mad,' laughed Grace-Ella. Then, remembering why she'd invited her friends over, she sighed. She'd decided that today she would reveal her secret. Her stomach churned, but she couldn't back out now. Taking a deep breath, she said, 'Before we go on your beetle hunt, there's something I want to tell you. But you must promise to keep it a secret. You can't tell anyone.'

'That sounds worrying,' said Fflur. 'You're not ill, are you? Or moving away?'

'No, nothing like that. Just promise first.'

Both Bedwyr and Fflur promised and waited for Grace-Ella to continue.

'Let's go in the summerhouse, I'll tell you in there.'

Once they were inside, Grace-Ella began.

'Well, I know this is going to sound completely crazy but … a few weeks ago … I found out that I'm … a witch.'

Bedwyr spluttered with laughter. 'Oh, Grace-Ella. You do crack me up.'

'It's not a joke, it's the truth,' she said.

'Oh, come off it,' said Fflur. 'You're not a witch. It's just another one of your batty ideas. Like when we decided that we were fairies and were going to live at the bottom of your garden.'

Grace-Ella shook her head. How was she going to prove to them that she was telling the truth?

'Hey, don't tell me, your dad's a wise old wizard,' said Bedwyr, chuckling.

'Actually it comes from Mam's side of the family,' corrected Grace-Ella.

'Your mam's a witch? Now that I can believe,' said Bedwyr.

Fflur gave him a nudge. 'Perhaps we should listen to the whole story.'

'Oh, come on, you don't think she's telling the truth? She's just gone completely Lady Gaga on us, that's all. Which is fine by me. Life's too short to be dull and boring, that's what Taid always says.'

'I know I sound completely cuckoo. I could barely believe it myself, but I swear it's the truth,' said Grace-Ella, looking pleadingly at her friends.

'Ok, let's say you are telling the truth,' said Fflur, 'what exactly does it mean, anyway? That you can fly around on a broomstick and cast spells?'

'I'm not sure about the flying on a broomstick bit yet,' answered Grace-Ella, 'but yes, I can cast spells.'

'Really. Show us then,' said Bedwyr.

'I'm only supposed to cast spells when I'm alone or with other witches, but I'm sure I can trust you and there'll be no harm done.'

Grace-Ella picked up her magic wand.

'Here goes,' she said, pointing her wand at the plate of Welsh cakes on the table. 'Up, up and away, fly into the air. With a swish and a swosh, land over there.'

She waved her wand in the air then pointed it at her friends. Slowly, the cakes rose from the plate, twirled in the air then landed in Bedwyr and Fflur's open hands.

'You … they … giddy goose,' stuttered
Bedwyr.

'Did that really just happen?' whispered
Fflur, wide-eyed.

Grace-Ella nodded. 'Now do you believe
me?'

The two bewildered friends stared at
Grace-Ella.

'Oh … my … google-doodle,' said

Bedwyr finally. 'You really are a witch? That's just bone-breakingly bonkers. And you called me mad! You're like Mademoiselle Mad. This is mammoth with a capital M.'

He suddenly started doing what can only be described as some sort of tribal dance around the room, whooping and waving his arms in the air. When he'd finished, Grace-Ella turned to Fflur, who was very quiet.

'It doesn't mean that I'm different. Not really. I'm still just me.'

A smile spread slowly across Fflur's face. 'A witch. And you can cast real spells. That's not crazy, that's amazingly fabulous.'

'I'm so glad you believe me,' said Grace-Ella, relieved. 'But you do promise to keep it a secret? And you do still want to be my friends?'

'Of course we do,' said Fflur, hugging her. 'I can't believe you'd think that we wouldn't. You've always been my best friend and nothing's going to change that.'

'You're actually stranger than me,' added Bedwyr, 'and that takes some doing. Besides, who else would help me look for bugs?'

'Phew, that's so great. I've been so worried about telling you. I don't know what I would have done if you hadn't wanted to be my friends anymore.'

'You silly old moo,' said Fflur. 'Who wouldn't want a real witch as a best friend? This is so cool. Can you show us some more magic?'

The three friends were soon rolling about laughing as books and boots and cups and coats came to life and went flying around the room. They ducked and chased the flying objects as their bottoms were kicked by boots and coats landed over their heads, making them stumble into each other. The summerhouse was a picture of magical mayhem.

At midday, Mrs Bevin called from the back door for Fflur and Grace-Ella to come in for lunch.

'I'd better go,' said Bedwyr. 'Don't want the Snootyius Ladyium catching me here or she'll start chasing me with her fly swatter again. Besides, I have to go into town to buy some new school shoes. Mam says I must sleep with my feet in a bag of compost, cos they don't stop growing. I'm a size eight already. Beetle-scrunchers, Taid calls them. Shame I can't get the hang of tying laces, mind. The lady in the shop always says, "A big boy like you should have learned to tie your laces by now."'

He sat on the floor to put on his boots, frowning in concentration as he tried to tie the laces. When he thought he'd got it, he pulled both ends, but they just fell open untied.

'Let me help you,' said Grace-Ella, pointing her wand at Bedwyr's boots. 'Loop and twist, under and through. Tie up the laces of this shoe.'

Bedwyr watched as his laces carefully tied themselves.

'The magic will stay on the laces till you've learnt how to tie them yourself. Just hold them and let your fingers follow what they do. You'll soon get the hang of it.'

Grace-Ella and Fflur waved goodbye to Bedwyr as he climbed over the fence chanting, 'Loop and twist, under and through. Loop and twist, under and through.'

'So now that you're a witch,' said Fflur as they walked to the house, 'does this mean that you can magic away Amelia?'

'Unfortunately not,' answered Grace-Ella.

'Oh well, but I bet we can have some great fun with your magic, can't we?'

'Well, there's definitely no rule in the book that says magic can't be used for fun,' said Grace-Ella, linking her arm through her friend's.

Chapter Nine
The Pumpkin Pie Disaster

'The annual Halloween party will be on Friday night,' Mrs Nag told the class on Monday morning. 'There'll be prizes for the best fancy dress costume and for St Winifred's "Dancing Diva".'

The classroom bubbled with excitement. The annual Halloween party was a highlight of the year and they couldn't wait for Friday night.

'I'll have the best costume,' boasted Amelia as the girls headed for their cookery lesson. 'I've won for the last two years. And this year, Mami's hiring a make-up artist so I'm going to look amazing and I'm so going to win.'

'She'd definitely win as a poisonous black widow spider,' Grace-Ella whispered to

Fflur.

The giggling pair caught Amelia's attention and she turned to glower at them.

'You two don't even need costumes. You're freaky enough just as you are.'

'Today we're going to prepare pumpkin pies,' said Mrs Bun, the cookery teacher. 'You'll work in pairs and the best pumpkin pie will be presented at the Halloween party.'

Grace-Ella and Fflur dashed off to their work area. Fflur often helped her mother to bake at home and was confident that they could produce a prize-winning pie.

'We could win this,' she said excitedly. 'That would really annoy Amelia.'

With the preparations done, Mrs Bun walked around for a quick examination before the pies were placed in the ovens.

'A little messy,' she said to Megan and

Catrin. 'I think your filling may well ooze out of the sides.'

Next she inspected Ceinwen and Amelia's pie.

'Very neat girls, a great effort. I hope it tastes as good as it looks.'

Ceinwen and Amelia smirked at the rest of the class.

Lastly, Mrs Bun walked over to Grace-Ella and Fflur. Fflur had done most of the preparation but Grace-Ella had decorated the top of the pie with pastry pumpkin shapes.

'What a wonderful-looking pie, girls, truly creative,' she said. 'The best preparation, I believe. Now into the ovens they go and when they're done I'll do the taste test before we decide on the winner.'

'This is going to be truly scrumptious,' said Fflur as Grace-Ella carefully placed the pie into the oven.

With their backs turned as they washed their dishes and cleared up, Grace-Ella and Fflur didn't notice Amelia slyly make her way over to their work area. Crouching down out of Mrs Bun's sight, she turned up the temperature dial on their oven to its highest setting.

As Grace-Ella turned to replace the clean chopping board on the top, she saw Amelia getting up off the floor.

'Just looking for my ring. I thought I saw it roll over here,' she said, before scurrying back to her own work area.

When the cleaning up was done, the class settled around the long table to write up their recipes.

'Remember to list all the ingredients and to write the method clearly and concisely,' said Mrs Bun, before pausing and sniffing the air.

The girls looked up from the table and watched as, like a sniffer dog, Mrs Bun prowled around the kitchen.

Stopping where Grace-Ella and Fflur had been working, she peered at the oven.

'What on earth…?'

She opened the oven door. A cloud of black smoke billowed out. Grabbing a tea towel, she wafted the smoke out of her eyes just as the smoke detector started to beep maniacally.

'Out to the yard everyone,' she spluttered

and coughed.

The girls rushed out to the schoolyard where Mrs Nag was standing, not looking too happy.

'It seems that there's been an incident in the kitchen,' she announced. 'Luckily, there has been no fire and no real damage. Perhaps the culprits will be willing to help Mrs Bun to clear up. The rest of you off to play.'

Grace-Ella and Fflur slowly made their way back to the kitchen.

'I don't understand,' said Fflur. 'I know I set the oven at the right temperature. I know I did.'

Mrs Bun was waiting for the girls in the kitchen, a little angry at the morning's disruption.

'That was a very careless thing to do, girls,' she said. 'You could have started a fire. You know we must always set the oven at the right temperature.'

'But, Miss —'

'No excuses, you have to be more careful. But I think you've learnt your lesson and you'll have to miss out on the competition this year.'

She pulled the pie out of the oven and dropped it onto the worktop. Grace-Ella and Fflur stared in horror at the blackened mess, the neat decorative pumpkin shapes now unrecognisable. The girls were baffled and felt utterly miserable.

'Wait a minute,' said Grace-Ella. 'When we were clearing up, Amelia came over here looking for her ring. I saw her getting up off the floor. Do you think…? No, she wouldn't, would she?'

The two friends locked eyes.

'Yes, she most certainly would,' seethed

Grace-Ella. 'She can't stand the thought of anyone doing better than her. What a … a … sneaky, slimy little snake. She's not going to get away with this!'

Back at Number 32 later that day, Grace-Ella told Mr Whiskins all about the pumpkin pie disaster.

'She really is a nasty piece of work, isn't she?' he said. 'She'll get her comeuppance one day. They say what comes around goes around, so don't you worry any more.'

But Grace-Ella did worry about it. It was so unfair that Amelia could be so mean and not get punished. She didn't know what to do. She certainly didn't want to break any of the Council's rules, but she also didn't want to let Amelia get away with being so horrid. Would teaching someone a lesson be classed as seeking revenge?

Chapter 10
Party Preparations

'I wish I could come to your Halloween party,' moaned Bedwyr on Thursday evening as he and Grace-Ella sat in the horse chestnut tree at the bottom of the garden. 'We never have one at our school and I'd love to get all dressed up like some kind of venomous spider or something. I bet you've got all sorts of magical things planned and I'll be missing out on it all. And Auntie Julie and Evan are coming over on Friday, so me and Evan will be sat in my room completely ignoring each other because we so don't get on. All he talks about is football and who's winning the prentice league or whatever it's called. Hey, maybe if I dressed as a witch you could smuggle me in...'

'Do you know,' said Grace-Ella, 'I think you're right. That's exactly what we should do.'

They jumped to the ground and landed in a messy heap.

'Come over tomorrow about five o'clock. I've plenty of costumes and I'm sure we can transform you into the best-looking witch at St Winifred's,' she said.

'If you say so,' said Bedwyr. 'I hadn't exactly planned on getting dressed up as a girl, but it does kind of sound fun. But even if you do manage to get me in, what about dancing? These beetle-scrunchers are great for stomping, but they aren't all girly-twirly. They'll see through my disguise straight away.'

'Leave it with me,' said Grace-Ella, a twinkle in her eye.

Back in her bedroom, Grace-Ella browsed through 'Potions: Part One' and stopped at the 'D' section.

'Aha,' she said. 'Just the thing. Come on, Mr Whiskins. We've got work to do.'

With the cauldron set up, she read out the ingredients.

'A handful of bird's feathers and a spoonful of honey ... some spidery webs and wobbly jelly ... a couple of pine cones to add some prickle and a pinch of glitter to add some sparkle.'

She stirred the ingredients and watched the liquid bubble to a sparkling silver.

'Now for the magic words: Twist and swirl and give it a whirl. A dancing delight to make you twirl.'

When the potion was ready, Grace-Ella carefully poured it into a glass bottle.

'Now I definitely know who's going to be

St Winifred's "Dancing Diva!"' she said.

'I'll go and get changed while you two sort your outfits out,' said Fflur the following evening, leaving Grace-Ella and Bedwyr in the summerhouse.

Pulling out her dressing-up box, Grace-Ella rummaged through. She found a pair of orange-and-black-striped tights, a purple tutu and a black top with green stars on it.

'Put these on to start with,' she said, passing the assortment of clothes to Bedwyr. 'I'll just go and get dressed with Fflur and then I'll add the final touches.'

'Are you serious?' he said, holding the purple tutu like it was a rotten old aubergine. 'I am going to look ridiculous with a capital R.'

When Grace-Ella got to her bedroom, Fflur

was already dressed in her cat costume.

'It's rubbish, isn't it?' she said glumly.
'I did try, but I'm just not very good at
making things. The others will laugh when
they see me. I'll be the biggest joke of the
night.'

Grace-Ella hated seeing her friend look
so miserable. But she had to agree, the
costume was a bit lacking in originality and
did look a little rushed.

The lumpy tail was made from a black
stocking stuffed with newspaper balls,
which had then been stapled to her black
leggings. The ears were triangles of flimsy
black card taped onto a hairband and were
already drooping. She had painted the end
of her nose black and put three long stripes
on each cheek as whiskers.

'Don't worry. I think I know what we can
do,' said Grace-Ella.

'What do you think?' asked Bedwyr as Grace-Ella and Fflur returned to the summerhouse.

'Witchtastic!' said Grace-Ella. 'Now, put this wig and hat on and I'll put a bit of face paint on you and no one will suspect a thing.'

Bedwyr pulled on the black wig and pointy witch's hat. Grace-Ella painted his face green, smudged black around his eyes

then dotted a couple of ugly warts on his nose and chin.

'Now give me your best pout so that I can paint your lips purple,' she said.

Bedwyr leaned forwards and puckered up his mouth. The brush tickled and he tried his best not to laugh, but ended up making hilarious raspberry noises which had Grace-Ella in giggles.

'Ta-dah!' she said when she was done. 'The wickedest witch in St Winifred's. Well, apart from Amelia that is.'

'Hubble, bubble, boil some trouble,' cackled Bedwyr as he looked in the mirror.

Grace-Ella turned her attention to Fflur. 'Now, let's see if we can get you looking a bit more like Mr Whiskins,' she said, picking up her magic wand.

'You are sure that you can un-cast the spell? As much as I like cats, I think I prefer to be human,' said Fflur a little nervously.

'Don't worry, I'll un-cast the spell after the party and you'll be back to normal. Now, just stand still. Twitchy, witchy when the moon comes out, a tail and whiskers you shall sprout.'

The magic wand sparked at Fflur, who was standing with her eyes shut tight. The three friends waited for something to happen.

'Oh, my face feels a little tingly,' said Fflur after a few seconds.

Grace-Ella and Bedwyr watched open-mouthed as out of Fflur's cheeks sprouted some long silky whiskers.

'Oh … um … my bottom's tingling now…'

She turned her head to look behind her. They stared in amazement as a long fluffy black tail began to grow. It grew longer and longer until it curled gracefully up her back.

Her nails changed next, transforming into cat-like claws. Her eyes took on a bright yellow glow and narrowed into a feline shape. The cardboard ears turned furry and twitched on her head.

'Oh … my … kitty-katkins,' remarked Bedwyr.

'Purrrfect,' purred Fflur, admiring herself in the mirror.

'Right, I think we're ready,' said Grace-Ella. 'Let's go. Oh, I nearly forgot. I just need to grab something.'

She hurried over to the shelves and pushed something into the pocket of her black cloak.

'What's that?' asked Bedwyr.

'You'll see,' she said winking.

Mrs Bevin was waiting for the children in the kitchen.

'Ready?' she asked. 'Oh, I thought it was only you and Fflur. You didn't mention any other friends.'

'Sorry, I forgot. This is um … Beatrice. She's new at school so I said she could come with us.'

Mrs Bevin peered closely at Bedwyr. 'You look familiar. Do I know your parents?'

'No, I don't think so,' said Grace-Ella. 'They've just moved here from … um…'

'Hungary,' said Fflur.

'Oh goodness, Fflur. You can't possibly be,' said Mrs Bevin. 'You've not long eaten tea. There'll be food at the party.'

'No, I'm not *hungry*,' Fflur explained. 'I said *Hungary*. Beatrice comes from Hungary.'

'Oh, I see. How wonderful. Well, Beatrice, you must tell your mum about our "Coffi Cymraeg" every Thursday morning. It's just a get together to help newcomers to learn some basic Welsh. We have a lot of fun and cake. She should come along and get to know some of us mothers from the school. Anyway, let's get going. Don't want you missing any of the party.'

Mrs Bevin looked suspiciously at Grace-Ella's magic wand as they left the house.

'I hope you're not planning any funny business,' she whispered.

'Wouldn't dream of it,' Grace-Ella answered.

Chapter 11
Spooks, Ghouls and Dancing Shoes

Lanterns hung from the trees at St Winifred's casting eerie shadows across the driveway. The school looked perfectly haunting under the dark night sky twinkling with stars and a full moon.

'Oh, great,' said Grace-Ella as they walked up to the school, 'a welcoming committee.'

Standing in the archway was Amelia and her friends. Amelia clearly wanted everyone to comment on her costume as soon as they arrived. She was dressed as a corpse bride; her hair had been sprayed silver and her face painted porcelain white with dark sunken eyes and ruby red lips. She wore a torn and tattered white wedding dress with a long veil. Her costume did look professional.

'Oh, you decided not to dress-up then, Gross-Ella,' Amelia said smirking. 'And you make a perfect fat cat, Fflur. And you…' She frowned at Bedwyr.

'Whoever you are, you look like some weird ballerina with some disgusting skin disease.'

Amelia and her friends cackled with laughter, like their very own witch's coven.

'Please can we sneak into her house one night and cast a shrinking spell on her so that I can keep her in a jar?' begged Bedwyr as they walked inside.

The school had been transformed. Candlelit pumpkins were placed in the windows, the glistening gossamer of spiders' webs hung from corners, bat bunting draped from the ceiling and spooks and ghouls were stuck onto the walls.

A selection of Halloween games had been set up – apple bobbing, hanging apples, pin the tail on the black cat and witch's stew. Soon the school hall was full of witches and cats and ghosts and ghouls. Mrs Nag, dressed in a long red dress, a black cloak with a large spiked collar and carrying a devil's fork, stalked around the room pointing her fork and ranting randomly. 'Don't spill your drink … not so loud, girls … no cheating…'

'Mrs Nag needs to lighten up,' said Fflur. 'This is a party. Surely she can stop her nagging just for tonight.'

The disco started with the 'Time Warp'. Miss Fitz, dressed as a not very scary pink fairy, flittered around urging everyone to dance. 'Come on, girls. Let's get the evening under way with the "Dancing Diva" contest.'

'There's no way that I'm getting up to

dance,' said Bedwyr. 'I can't possibly twirl about like you lot.'

'Don't worry,' said Grace-Ella. 'I've prepared a little something for you.' She pulled the bottle of Dancing Delight out of her pocket. 'I'll just sprinkle this onto your shoes and let the magic do its work. You'll be a real "Dancing Diva".'

'Ok, let's do it,' said Bedwyr excitedly, taking a seat and sticking his feet out.

Grace-Ella unscrewed the lid and was about to pour the potion onto Bedwyr's shoes when Amelia, overly-exuberant in her mission to win the contest, spun into Grace-Ella, knocking the potion clean out of her hands.

'Out of the way,' she snapped as she flung her veil back over her shoulders and continued her enthusiastic pirouetting around the room.

'Never mind,' said Bedwyr. 'I'll just sit here and watch and hope that the scary pink fairy doesn't pounce on me and drag me off.'

But Grace-Ella didn't hear. She watched in horror as the open bottle landed on the table. The potion seeped onto the cloth and dripped over the side, right onto the unsuspecting Mrs Nag's shoes.

It didn't take long for Mrs Nag's foot to start tapping.

'What on earth?'

Her foot took on a life of its own and started to tap out towards the dance floor. Mrs Nag, looking very uneasy, grabbed onto the edge of the table and tried to drag her leg back. But it was no use. Her arms flailed into the air and started waving about.

Unable to control her body, she sashayed and swayed into the middle of the room and was soon doing a very energetic 'Time Warp'. The girls, spotting their usually stern

teacher, stopped still and stared.

Song after song played and Mrs Nag continued to dance like she'd never danced before. She mashed to the 'Monster Mash', galloped around shouting, 'Who are you going to call?' with the *Ghostbusters* theme and demonstrated some tremendous twists and turns for 'Thriller'.

Finally, the music stopped and the lights were turned on. Mrs Nag, whose dancing frenzy stopped as soon as the music did, stood in the centre of the room looking completely dazed, unable to believe what had just happened.

Miss Fitz, staring in wonder at her colleague, made her way up to the stage.

'It's time to announce the winner of the "Dancing Diva" contest,' she said into the microphone. 'This year, the result is a little different and I think you'll all agree that there was one truly outstanding dancer, so I'm proud to announce that this year, St Winifred's "Dancing Diva" trophy goes to … Mrs Nag.'

The room remained in stunned silence for a few seconds. Then slowly, the clapping began. It increased to a loud crescendo with lots of whoops and cheers. Looking completely bewildered, Mrs Nag walked unsteadily onto the stage to accept her prize.

'Um … thank you very much, Miss Fitz … um … I'm not sure what came over me. I hope you're all enjoying the evening … I … um … certainly seem to be. Anyway, it's time for the judging of your costumes so if you'd like to take part, stand in a line and Miss Fitz and I will walk around. There's a prize for the top three.'

Forgetting about their dancing teacher,

the girls pushed and shoved to form a line.

'Spread my veil out,' Amelia ordered her friends. 'And don't stand too close to me.'

Miss Fitz and Mrs Nag (still flushed and a little disorientated) walked up and down the line of girls. After conferring quietly at the foot of the stage, Mrs Nag was ready to announce the results.

'Right. We've chosen the top three. Well done to all of you, there are many excellent costumes. But I must say, there is one that really stands out and choosing the winner has been very easy for Miss Fitz and me.'

Beaming, Amelia flicked her hair over her shoulder.

'So we'll start with the third prize, which goes to … Jessica.'

The others clapped as Jessica walked onto the stage to collect her prize money.

'The second prize goes to … Amelia.'

Amelia was busy fluffing out her veil, not yet listening to Mrs Nag as she was only waiting for the announcement of the winner.

'Go on, you came second,' said Ceinwen, nudging her best friend.

Amelia flinched. 'What? They must have announced it wrong. I can't possibly have come second.'

'Amelia, please come up for your prize,' said Mrs Nag impatiently.

Amelia marched onto the stage and snatched the envelope from Mrs Nag before rushing off to her friends for their condolences.

'And the first prize, for the most realistic costume Miss Fitz and I have ever seen, goes to … Fflur Penri.'

'Me?' said Fflur.

'Yes, you,' laughed Grace-Ella. 'Go on, go

and get your prize.'

Fflur, who had never won anything in her entire life, felt like she was floating onto the stage. She bowed gracefully then took her prize from Mrs Nag. Grace-Ella and Bedwyr whistled and cheered as Fflur walked back to them.

'Thank you, Grace-Ella,' Fflur said, hugging her friend. 'The three of us can share the prize money. We'll go to the cinema or something. I feel a bit bad though, like I cheated.'

'You didn't cheat. Amelia had a helping hand from a make-up artist. You had a helping hand from a witch.'

'Now before we tuck into the food,' continued Mrs Nag, 'Mrs Bun would like to announce the winner of the pumpkin pie contest.'

'Yes, after a slightly disastrous lesson, I

can now reveal that the best pumpkin pie was baked by … Amelia and Ceinwen.'

Amelia, forgetting her disappointment at the fancy dress contest, flounced onto the stage. Grabbing the microphone out of Mrs Bun's hands, she said, 'Thank you so much. I'm sure you'll all enjoy my pie and will agree that my pie is the best pie you've ever tasted.'

Then she pushed Ceinwen back down the

steps before she'd even had the chance to climb up.

With the music back on, Grace-Ella, Fflur and Bedwyr headed over to the food table. They couldn't wait to tuck into the ghoulish buffet.

There were creepy cupcakes topped with eyeballs and spiders, messy meringue ghosts, disgusting vegetable fingers to dip in scream cheese, skull-shaped sandwiches, black liquorice bats, slimy worm jelly sweets and of course the prize-winning pumpkin pie.

'Shame you wasted all that money on hiring a make-up artist,' Grace-Ella said as she stood next to Amelia.

She glared firstly at Grace-Ella, then at Fflur, then at Bedwyr. With her eyes narrowed, she stared at Bedwyr, from the tip of his hat to the tip of his toes, frowning at his particularly large feet.

'I have my eye on you lot, Grace-Ella. I don't trust you one bit. I know that you and that fat cat cheated somehow. And there's something very suspicious-looking about you,' she said, prodding Bedwyr in his chest.

'Erm … I think you've got an eye on yourself actually,' said Fflur, staring at the cupcake on Amelia's plate.

Amelia screamed as the eyeball cake topper on her plate swivelled from side to side then winked at her. The eyeball went flying through the air as she dropped her plate in fright, and it landed with a splash in Mrs Bun's cup of tea.

Within seconds, the whole hall erupted into screams and squeals. The plastic spiders dropped from the cakes and scurried around; the jelly worms began

wriggling and writhing and the vegetable
dipping fingers tapped along the tables. The
apples in the 'apple-bobbing' bowls bobbed
frantically, splashing water onto the floor.

'What on earth's happening?' whispered
Fflur.

'Um … I think it might be my fault,' said
Grace-Ella. 'I think the Dancing Delight
potion that I prepared for Bedwyr got onto
the food when Amelia knocked it out of my
hands.'

The three friends watched as a very flustered Mrs Nag tried in vain to reassure the hysterical girls.

'Calm down, girls,' she shouted over the music, 'this is ridiculous. Stop throwing your food —'

She slipped in a puddle of water and landed on her bottom just as a messy meringue ghost came hurtling through the air and splattered into her face.

'That's enough,' she shouted as she wiped the cream from her nose and eyes. 'Mrs Bun, Miss Fitz will you help to get things under control…'

But poor Miss Fitz was standing trembling on a chair, petrified as spiders scuttled across the floor. And as for Mrs Bun, she was frantically flicking through her recipe books to see what on earth she had done wrong.

The Halloween party had turned into complete chaos. Drinks and food flew from one end of the hall to the other, showering the girls and their teachers with a sticky, spooky mess. They slipped and slid as they ran about in panic, landing on top of each other.

Ceinwen's prize-winning pumpkin pie landed right on her head. Squealing, she ran around blindly, bumping into chairs and tables.

'Come on,' said Grace-Ella to her friends. 'Let's get out of here till the spell wears off.'

Amelia, who had been hiding in the toilets, not wanting her costume ruined by the flying food, saw the three friends hurry away down the corridor. Suspecting they were up to something and now certain that the mysterious friend was that bug-boy who lived next door to Grace-Ella, she followed, eager to catch them red-handed and get them into trouble.

Chapter 12
Fright Night

'Don't turn around, but I think we're being followed,' Grace-Ella whispered. 'And I bet I know who it is. Quick, in here.'

They ducked into the library and hid behind one of the bookshelves.

Peeking through the books, they watched Amelia creep into the room. She tiptoed slowly around, crouching to peer between the shelves.

'I know you're in here, Grace-Ella. And I know that your mysterious friend is your disgusting bug boyfriend. Just you wait till I tell Mrs Nag that you've brought a boy here. You're going to be in so much trouble. I bet you won't be allowed out at break for the whole term. Actually, you'll probably get expelled for breaking the rules.'

Fflur and Bedwyr looked worriedly at Grace-Ella. Grace-Ella clenched her fists as her anger brewed inside. Amelia was forever being horrible and never getting punished. She thought she could get away with anything. It was so unfair. But how could she teach Amelia a lesson? How could she show her that she couldn't behave like this?

Amelia grinned. 'And I shall definitely insist that Fatty Fflur is disqualified from the dressing-up competition. That'll serve you right.'

Unable to take any more, Grace-Ella signalled to Fflur and Bedwyr to stay where they were and stepped out from her hiding place. She wasn't sure what she was going to do, but she had to do something. She wished that Mr Whiskins was there to help her, but this was something she was going to have to face by herself.

'What have you got to say for yourself?' demanded Amelia. 'I'm right, aren't I? You have brought that boy here.' Smiling, she began chanting. 'Grace-Ella loves the stupid smelly bug-boy.'

Grace-Ella was furious. How dare Amelia stand there making fun of her and her friends and expect her to just take it!

'Do you know, Amelia, I've had about enough of your nasty, horrid, mean mouth. You're always picking on me and Fflur and you think that you're better than everyone at this school. You're even mean to your own friends. I don't know why they bother with you. You're nothing but a nasty bully.'

'What's got into you this evening? A bit prickly, aren't you,' smirked Amelia.

'You're not going to get away with it for ever. What goes around comes around,' said

Grace-Ella, thinking back to Mr Whiskins'
words.

Amelia yawned exaggeratedly. 'Oh, really.
And what exactly are you and Fatty Fflur
going to do? Is she going to smother me
in chocolate and eat me?' Amelia smiled.
'Face it, Grace-Ella. There is nothing you
can do to stop me.'

Grace-Ella's fingers curled tightly around
the wand in her cloak pocket. Her heart
began to race. Could she do this? Could she
use her magic to stop Amelia?

'You're a nasty piece of work and it's about
time someone taught you a lesson,' she said,
pulling out the wand.

'What are you going to do now? Cast
a spell on me and turn me into a toad?'
laughed Amelia. 'You're such a loser, Gross-
Ella.'

That was it! Grace-Ella was not going to

be ridiculed by Amelia any more. She was going to show her that there was something she could do. Something she was good at. She might not be able to put a spell on Amelia – rule two – but she could put a spell on the library…

Taking a deep breath and mustering up every ounce of courage she had, Grace-Ella waved her wand in the air and with a tremor in her voice, spoke the magic words, 'Vampire bats and witches' hats, give us a howl and a scream. Ghosts and ghouls come out to play, tonight on Halloween.'

Amelia sniggered. 'You're such a weirdo. I suppose you think you're a real witch —'

The library door slammed shut, making Amelia jump. Holding her hand steady, Grace-Ella pointed her wand at one of the bookshelves. A book flew into the air, landing at Amelia's feet. As she bent to pick

it up, another one landed with a thud next to her … then another … then another. She turned her head this way and that, as book after book flew through the air.

'I've had enough of your stupid games,' said Amelia, beginning to look uneasy. 'I'm going to get Mrs Nag. You wait till she sees this mess.'

Shoving Grace-Ella out of the way, she pulled on the door handle. It didn't budge.

'Open this door right now,' she snapped.

Feeling braver every second, Grace-Ella looked around the room. What could she do next?

She pointed her wand at the chandelier hanging from the ceiling. It began to sway dramatically. The room went dark. The light of the full moon shining in through the windows gave the library a shadowy glow.

Panicked, Amelia tried to turn on the lights, but nothing happened.

'I don't know how you're doing this, but I want you to stop right now,' she said, her eyes darting around the room.

'Stop? You want me to stop? What about all the times I've asked you to stop being nasty to me and Fflur? Have you ever listened? Have you ever stopped? No, you haven't. And I'm not stopping either. I'm just getting started.'

She scanned the room again. Settling on the fireplace, she pointed her wand and out flew a cloud of bats. Amelia covered her head with her arms.

'Help! Get me out of here!' she screamed as she pounded on the door with her fists.

But Grace-Ella was determined to teach Amelia a lesson, once and for all.

'You think being mean and horrid is something to be proud of,' she said. 'But upsetting everyone doesn't make you look clever. Picking on others doesn't make you smart and strong. You're the loser, Amelia.'

Feeling more in control than she'd ever been in Amelia's company, she spun in a circle and waved her wand in the air. The library's sash windows shot open and started to bang up and down. The painting above the fireplace of the school's founding headmistress swayed from side to side. The chandelier creaked as it swung to and fro. Books somersaulted through the air. The bats flapped wildly around the room. Amelia yelled and frantically shook the door handle.

'I did warn you, Amelia,' said Grace-Ella. 'I did tell you that you wouldn't get away with being horrid for ever.'

Hearing Mrs Nag's heels click-clacking down the corridor, Grace-Ella quickly slipped her wand back in her pocket and clicked her fingers three times to uncast the spells. She hid behind the shelves with her two friends. She was shaking – using all that magic had really taken it out of her. She was thrilled it had worked and was certain that Amelia would think twice before being nasty from now on.

But what was going to happen? Was she going to be in trouble? Was Mrs Nag going to find out what she'd done and have her expelled? What would her mam say? She'd probably get grounded for the rest of her life at least. And what about the Witch Council? She hadn't broken a rule … had she?

Mrs Nag was sure to find them cowering behind the bookshelf once Amelia told her what had happened. What were they going to do?

Grace-Ella quickly decided. 'Listen. We can't get caught. We'll be in huge trouble. There's nowhere to hide in here. There's a shrinking spell I know … well, I've never actually tried it but I don't think we have a choice. Are you ready?'

Fflur and Bedwyr nodded nervously. Grace-Ella raised her magic wand. 'Wave my wand with a blink and a wink, tap three times and make us shrink.'

With a spark from the wand, the three
friends shrunk to the size of furry hamsters
and hopped up to hide on top of the books,
just as the library door flew open. Amelia
fell into the corridor, landing at Mrs Nag's
feet. She grabbed onto her teacher's ankles.

'Good grief, Amelia. Whatever's the
matter with you?'

'Save me … please … Grace-Ella … a

witch … casting spells…'

'What are you talking about?' asked Mrs Nag.

'Grace-Ella … a witch…'

'Amelia, I often praise you for your imagination when you're writing stories, but I think you're letting it run a little wild this evening.'

'No … in there … Grace-Ella … she's a witch.' She clung tighter to Mrs Nag's legs.

'Amelia Cadwallader, please let go of me and get up off the floor. I've had quite enough nonsense this evening.'

Mrs Nag hauled Amelia up onto her feet.

'But look … in there … bats and books everywhere… It was Grace-Ella, she's a witch…'

'That's enough,' Mrs Nag said, turning on the light in the library. 'Look, there's nothing in here. Grace-Ella is over in the gym with all the others, I expect. I've sent everyone over there to clean up before your parents arrive. Whatever's got into you?'

Stepping slowly into the room, Amelia saw that the books were standing neatly on the shelves; the windows were shut tight; the chandelier and the painting were hanging still, and there wasn't a bat or Grace-Ella in sight.

'But … I swear … I'm telling the truth…' she stuttered.

'Not another word, Amelia. I don't want to hear any more of this ridiculous nonsense. There are no such things as witches and I expect better from you. Now hurry along to the gym. I've had quite enough for one night!'

With that, she marched back down the corridor, Amelia trailing quickly behind. Clicking her fingers three times to undo the

spell, Grace-Ella, Fflur and Bedwyr
returned to their normal size.

'I can't believe I made the shrinking spell
work,' said Grace-Ella.

'You are amazingly amazing,' said Bedwyr.

Fflur looked a little worried.

'What's the matter?' Grace-Ella asked.
'We did it. We taught Amelia a lesson. You
should be smiling.'

'But I think she had a real fright,' said
Fflur. 'Do you think she'll be OK?'

'Oh, don't worry,' Grace-Ella said. 'She'll
be back to her old self on Monday. But
perhaps she won't be so mean to us now
that she thinks I'm a real witch.'

'Weren't you supposed to keep it a secret?'
asked Bedwyr. 'Once Amelia gets over her
shock, she'll blurt it out to everyone.'

'Who's going to believe her? How can she
prove it? You heard Mrs Nag. There are no

such things as witches.'

Grace-Ella smiled. It didn't look like she was going to get into trouble after all. And she was sure that she hadn't broken any of the Council's rules. She felt proud of herself for finally having been brave enough to stand up to the school bully.

'Well, witch or not,' said Fflur, 'you're the best friend anyone could magic up.'

'Come on,' said Grace-Ella, 'I know a clean-up spell to sort the hall out before they come back from the gym.'

One by one the girls left the party to meet their waiting parents. The excitable chatter was incessant as they said how St Winifred's must be haunted. The quietest girl was Amelia, who was standing trembling at the front entrance, glancing back at the library and jumping with every little sound.

When the girls had gone safely home, Mrs Nag and the other teachers returned to the hall to get started on cleaning up. But to their astonishment, they found that the floor was gleaming; the food had been placed in the bins and the bags tied up ready to be taken out; the tables had been wiped clean; the chairs were all stacked neatly against the walls and the decorations had all been taken down and were packed into their boxes.

'I can't believe my eyes,' said Mrs Nag. 'Tonight has been the strangest Halloween ever.'

Chapter 13
A Witch's Life

Monday morning dawned bright and crisp. The school week bustled by and the excitement of the previous Friday slowly began to fade. Amelia tried to convince everyone that Grace-Ella was a witch, but no one believed her and they quickly tired of hearing her. Not wanting everyone to think that she was silly, Amelia finally gave up, but made sure that she kept out of Grace-Ella's way.

Mrs Nag seemed to have a new spring in her step and would give a jaunty little hop and skip when walking down the corridor. Grace-Ella could have sworn that she heard her humming 'Monster Mash' to herself as she followed her up the driveway one morning.

It seemed that a touch of magic had done St Winifred's the world of good.

On Saturday evening, Penelope Pendle once again made an unexpected appearance in Grace-Ella's bedroom.

'Good evening. I've just dropped by to check that everything is going as it should be.' She peered over the rim of her glasses at Grace-Ella. Grace-Ella swallowed. Did Penelope Pendle hold her gaze for a second longer than was normal? 'And to inform you about your first witch camp.'

She took a notepad and pen from her cloak pocket.

'Now, first things first. How are you getting along with your cat? Is it a good working partnership?'

Grace-Ella adored Mr Whiskins and couldn't imagine life without him.

'Oh yes,' she said. 'He's perfect. He's very helpful and we have lots of fun together. He's the best cat I could ever have wished for.'

'Good. Then Mr Whiskins shall remain as your black cat. That saves a lot of time and bother. We do have some witch-cat partnerships that, well, how should I put it … are highly mismatched. Only last week, we had a cat feed his witch a potion that turned her into a mouse and he gobbled her up. It was quite a palaver to retrieve the poor girl.'

She scribbled quickly on the notepad. 'Secondly, have you worked your way carefully through "Spells for Beginners?"'

'I've tried every spell and have managed to make each one work,' Grace-Ella said.

'Excellent. And you have been casting them correctly? In private?'

Once again she peered directly at Grace-Ella, who began to feel a little nervous. She was still certain that she hadn't broken any of the Council's rules, yet Penelope Pendle's stare was making her uneasy. Grace-Ella nodded slowly.

'Hm hm...' said Penelope Pendle as she scribbled once again on the notepad. 'If you pass the "Spells for Beginners" test at witch camp, you can move on to "Intermediate Spells", which will of course be far more powerful and will need greater care. Now thirdly, how are you managing your potions?'

'No major hiccups ... oh ... well ... perhaps one or two needed a little tweaking, but mostly they've been successful as well.'

'Splendid. Everything seems to be ship-shape here, which is what we like at the

Academy.'

She closed the notepad and placed it back in her pocket. 'You do always keep the Council's rules in mind, I'm sure. Because it's so easy to forget sometimes … to get swept along in the excitement of a situation. Always remember that breaking the rules will have consequences.' She paused. Grace-Ella held her breath. Was she about to get punished? 'And we wouldn't want that to happen. Not when everything seems to be going so well.'

Grace-Ella shook her head.

'Excellent. Perhaps re-reading some of the case studies in the book would be a good idea. It's always good to refresh the memory. But like I said, everything seems to be in order here and I think you're ready for Witch Camp. You'll receive a letter with all the details in the next few days and a map with directions. Any questions?'

Grace-Ella wanted to ask what would happen if she failed her tests at Witch Camp. She couldn't help but worry as she was so used to failing her tests in school. But before she had a chance to speak, Penelope Pendle had once again disappeared in a puff of purple smoke.

'Do you think she was hinting that I'd almost broken the rules?' Grace-Ella asked Mr Whiskins after Penelope Pendle had vanished. 'It seemed like that to me. But she can't possibly know that I've told Bedwyr and Fflur, can she?'

Mr Whiskins stretched and yawned. 'I think you're worrying about nothing.'

'But it was like she was trying to say something, wasn't it? And I remember you once warned me to beware that there could be eyes and ears lurking everywhere. Maybe they have a way of seeing everything I do. I mean, they are the cleverest witches in the world.'

'If she thought you'd broken the rules she would have said so and she would have given you a proper warning. She was just giving you a friendly reminder, that's all.'

'Maybe,' said Grace-Ella, feeling a little better. 'Anyway, you'll be coming to Witch Camp with me, won't you?'

'Of course,' he replied. 'We cats need to meet up every now and again as well.'

'I'm looking forward to going, but I'm a bit scared as well. I hope I do OK. I really don't want to be a failure. I wonder if I'll make any new friends there?' She settled down in bed, wondering what adventures awaited her at Witch Camp.

Being a witch had changed Grace-Ella's life. She had the pet that she'd always longed for. She had managed to do something that her mother was proud of. She was actually enjoying learning something new and now that Amelia was leaving her alone, school wasn't such a dread anymore. And she was having the most fun that she'd ever had in her life.

Yes, a witch's life was definitely the one for Grace-Ella.

Sharon Marie Jones grew up in mountainous North Wales. As a child, she listened in wide-eyed wonderment to local tales about giants and had her very own fairy door on the crab apple tree at the bottom of the garden. She is Mam to three boys and worked as a Primary School teacher for twelve years, before finally allowing herself to pursue that magical dream of becoming an author. She now happily gazes out of the window and writes full time.

*

Adribel was born in Argentina. She has lived in Granada in Spain since 1995 with her husband, son, daughter, two dogs, a guinea pig, a little bird, and several fish.

She has always drawn. When she decided on a career she chose architecture — she was wrong! Because she wanted tell stories. So she abandoned that, and began to study drawing humorous cartoons and caricatures in Buenos Aires. That's where she found her strengths: the line, the design of characters and her humour.

Adribel loves telling stories. As ideas often come at unexpected moments, she always keeps paper and pencils in her pockets, at home or in the car. She sometimes jots down a few words or a sketch, but usually both.